W9-BIB-213

MERMIN™

BOOK TWO: THE BIG CATCH

MERMIN™

BOOK TWO: THE BIG CATCH

Written and illustrated by
Joey Weiser

Edited by
Jill Beaton

Designed by
Keith Wood

Oni Press, Inc.
publisher, Joe Nozemack
editor in chief, James Lucas Jones
art director, Keith Wood
director of publicity, John Schork
director of sales, Cheyenne Allott
editor, Jill Beaton
editor, Charlie Chu
digital pre-press lead, Troy Look
graphic designer, Jason Storey
administrative assistant, Robin Herrera

1305 SE Martin Luther King Jr. Blvd.
Suite A
Portland, OR 97214

onipress.com
facebook.com/onipress
twitter.com/onipress
onipress.tumblr.com
tragic-planet.com

First Edition: November 2013
ISBN: 978-1-62010-101-8
Library of Congress Control Number: 2012953664

10 9 8 7 6 5 4 3 2 1

Printed in China.

CHAPTER ONE

BIRDS ALL OVER THE LACE AND PERTS SAY
A REMOT ISLAND
AN NNING OUND
LOO AT HOU
M ES

...BIZARRE INCIDENT AT TEAWATER ELEMENTARY LAST WEEK...
NE

HM?

REPORTERS RUSHED TO THE SCENE AS WHAT

RIGHT THERE!

II PAUSE

I THINK I FOUND SOMETHING!

MMMMNNNGGH!!

...

RGH!!!

MMM...

HMMMMMM

MNNNNNGGG

GGRRGHHH!!!

ACHEM!

NOTHING?
...

YOU DID MAKE SOME REAL GOOD FACES!
I'M SORRY, PETE. THE PSYCHIC CONNECTION IS ONLY BETWEEN MERMIN AND CREATURES OF THE SEA!
SIGH

BUT IT HAPPENED THE OTHER NIGHT! I SWEAR!

IT'S TRUE!
HMMM...

ANYWAY... C'MON, MERMIN. IT'S TIME FOR SCHOOL...

I-I REALLY MUST INSIST THAT I COME WITH YOU!

N-O-WAY!

TH-THE WHOLE REASON WHY I'M HERE IS TO KEEP WATCH OVER MERMIN, AND REPORT BACK TO OUR KINGDOM--

SERIOUSLY. ONE FISH-BOY AT SCHOOL IS BAD ENOUGH.

SORRY, BENNI! YOU HEARD THE BOSS!

TEAWATER ELEMENTARY
CLASS BEGINS IN TEN MINUTES, CHILDREN!
HELLO LITTLE FISHIES!

MERMIN! MERMIN! WE FOUND YOU!!

PSH! WHERE HAVE YOU BEEN?

ALL THAT STUFF IS OVER NOW...

WHY DON'CHA INTRODUCE ME TO YOUR GIRLFRIENDS, FISH-FACE!?

THEY AREN'T MY...
Oh, SORRY! I MEANT YOUR BOYFRIENDS!

C'MON, RANDY! DON'T YOU HAVE ANYTHING BETTER TO DO THAN PICK ON THE NEW KID?

NOBODY ASKED YOU TO BUTT IN, PENNY!
SO WHAT?

OKAY KIDS. TO YOUR SEATS...

TRY NOT TO LET RANDY BOTHER YOU...

THAT GUY COULDN'T EVEN TELL IF THOSE FISH WERE BOYS OR GIRLS!

LEARN

SO, DID YOU SEE THE NEW "GARGANTURA VS. TORGO" TRAILER?

YEAH!

LOOKS
REAT!
poke

HM?

. . .

"GO"

"AWAY."

"NOPE"

HEY MERMIN! WHATCHA LOOKIN' AT??

WHU? uh--I, WELL...

Nuh...NOTHING...

SO...

...WHAT'S UP, PENNY? IS LAUREL'S TABLE FULL...?

NO, HA HA! I DON'T ALWAYS SIT THERE!

LOOK, I DON'T HAVE ANYTHING TO TALK TO YOU GUYS ABOUT YOUR MONSTER MOVIE TOYS OR WHATEVER...

HOW ABOUT THIS? WE SHOULD ALL GO TO THE LIBRARY DOWNTOWN AFTER SCHOOL TODAY!

"THE LIBRARY?"

SURE! MY FRIENDS AND I GO THERE TO JUST HANG OUT, WATCH DVDs, READ COMICS AND MAGAZINES...

Oh, I DUNNO... WHAT DO YOU THINK PETE
LET'S DO IT!!!

YOU SHOULD BRING THAT FRIEND OF YOURS TOO!

The Shop

WELL! HERE WE ARE!

I DON'T SEE WHY WE DIDN'T JUST START BY LOOKING AT THE SCHOOL, AGENT BIRD!
TOO OBVIOUS!
JUST WHAT THEY'D EXPECT!

"THEY" AREN'T "EXPECTING" US AT ALL!
FOOD

LISTEN, AGENT SMITT, WHEN WE CATCH THIS THING WE DON'T WANT IT ON GOVERNMENT PROPERTY!

Oh FER...
LAST THING WE NEED IS THE FEDS INVOLVED!

Oh! I'M PICKING SOMETHING UP!
BEEP
BEEP

BEEP
BEEP
BEEP
BEEP
BEEP
BEEP

BEEP!
BEEP!
BEEP!
BEEP!
BEEP!
BEEP!
BEEP!
BEEP!
BEEP!

. . .
. . .

HOW WOULD YOU CLASSIFY YOUR URANIUM CONSUMPTION RECENTLY, YOUNG MAN?

uh...ABOUT AVERAGE, I GUESS?
Mm.

Eh?

TEAWATER LIBRA

AGENT BIRD!
NOT NOW, SMITT! I'M MAKING ADJUSTMENTS TO MY--

FORGET THAT! COME WITH ME!

MERMIN! THIS IS ONE OF MY FAVORITE COMICS, "SPACE PRINCE LANDED!"
Hmm...
IT'S ABOUT A PRINCE FROM OUTER SPACE WHO LANDS ON EARTH AND IS ALL MAD BECAUSE EVERYONE THINKS HE'S JUST A REGULAR KID! THEN HE SAVES THE WORLD FROM SOME OTHER ALIENS...

IT'S AWESOME!

A PRINCE, huh...?

YOU KNOW, THE SON OF THE KING!
THE ONE TO INHERIT THE KINGDOM!

RIGHT... YEAH...
JUST LIKE YOU, MERMIN!

WHAT!? NO!! BENNI!!!

"THE SON OF THE KING"...

"THE ONE TO INHERIT THE KINGDOM!" THIS IS A DIFFERENT SITUATION!!
B-BUT... MERMIN...

ARGH! WHO ASKED YOU, ANYWAY!?!

WAIT... WHAT?

CHAPTER TWO

WHAT??? IS THAT TRUE!? SERIOUSLY!?!
MERMIN, WHAT DO YOU MEAN, "PRINCE?"

I DIDN'T SAY "PRINCE!" THAT WAS BENNI!
OKAY, THEN. BENNI WHAT ARE YOU TALKING ABOUT?

I-I'M SORRY MERMIN! I D-DIDN'T REALIZE THAT YOU, uh, THAT YOU HADN'T TOLD THEM...

THERE'S NOTHING **TO** TELL!
MERMIN...

OH BOY! **ANYWAY!** WHAT A GREAT BOOK!

MERMIN, C'MON... WHAT'RE YOU--

LESSEE WHAT'S OUT THIS WINDOW! ♪DUM DUM DUM♫
HEY!! IT'S CLAIRE!!!

THERE SHE IS! HEY! CLAIRE!!

WHAT'S UP? HOW'S IT GOIN'??

GET OUT OF HERE! I'M NOT BABYSITTING TODAY!
WE'RE NOT BABIES!

OKAY, YEAH. BUT OUR CLUB MEETING IS TOMORROW. TODAY I'M HANGING OUT WITH MY FRIENDS!

BESIDES, I DON'T WANT TO GET INTO THE WHOLE "FISH BOY" THING WITH THEM...
TOO LATE.

CLAIRE, DO YOU KNOW THIS LITTLE GREEN KID??
YOU NEVER TOLD US ABOUT HIM!

HE'S JUST MY LITTLE BROTHER'S FRIEND!
WHEE!

NOW, SHOO!

TARGET: LOCATED! NO QUESTION!

WELL, KEEP TABS ON IT! I'M PREPPING OUR EQUIPMENT!
NO TIME! THEY'RE ON THE MOVE!
THAT'S WHY I SAID TO KEEP TABS ON--
I MAY HAVE TO
AAUUGH!!!
AGENT SMITT! AGENT SMITT! STATUS REPORT! DO YOU NEED BACK UP!?! AGENT SMITT!!

MAN! CLAIRE IS SO DUMB!

IT'S OKAY TOBY...
SORRY IF WE'RE NOT AS COOL AS HER STUPID FRIENDS!

I LIKED HER FRIENDS!

BUT THEY DID SAY I WAS "SICK" AND "WICKED"...THAT DIDN'T SEEM VERY NICE...

WHAT WAS THAT ABOUT A "CLUB MEETING"?

SORRY. "MEMBERS ONLY"...

SPEAKING OF THE CLUB, WHERE WILL WE MEET NOW THAT THE "CLUB HQ" IS DEMOLISHED?
SIGH

GOOD QUESTION...
Y'KNOW...

I KNOW OF A GREAT SPOT THAT COULD BE, LIKE, A "TEMPORARY HQ"...

I COULD SHOW YOU... IF I WERE A MEMBER...

uh...
WHY NOT?

OKAY PENNY!
WELL... LET'S SEE THE PLACE, THEN MAYBE...
?
psst!

PSST! HEY! CREATURE!!

ME?

YEAH, YOU! C'MERE!

OKAY! WHY?
JUST COME AROUND THE CORNER!

?

HA!!!...

GOTCHA!!!

I'VE GOT YOU NOW!

SHRIP!

TH-THAT WAS TRIPLE-REINFORCED POLY--
HA HA! I'VE HEARD ABOUT YOU "FISHER MEN" BEFORE!

SORRY! I'M DIFFERENT FROM WHAT YOU'RE SUPPOSED TO CATCH!

NO HARD FEELINGS!

HEY GUYS! WAIT UP!!

CHAPTER THREE

WOOOOOAAAAAHH...

THIS PLACE IS AWESOME!

YEAH! THERE'RE SOME BOATS AND STUFF AT THIS OLD DOCK, BUT I NEVER SEE ANYONE HERE!

THERE CERTAINLY IS A LOT OF COOL JUNK HERE...

MM...

MERMIN...I CAN'T STOP THINKING ABOUT WHAT YOU AND BENNI WERE SAYING IN THE LIBRARY...

...ON SECOND THOUGHT... MAYBE WE DON'T WANT TO GET INTO THIS... Y'KNOW...

(...around Penny...)

HEY!

DON'T THINK THAT I DON'T KNOW WHAT'S GOIN' ON OVER THERE!!

I'M PART OF THE CLUB NOW!
I HAVE EVERY RIGHT TO KNOW ABOUT MERMIN!

SORRY, PENNY, I GUESS--
WELL, THE CLUB THING HASN'T BEEN DECIDED... um, OFFICIALLY...

WHAT!? COME ON! I SHOWED YOU GUYS THIS COOL SPOT FOR THE NEW HQ!

IT'S NOTHING PERSONAL... LOOK, A LOT OF CRAZY STUFF HAS HAPPENED, AND I'M NOT SURE HOW MANY PEOPLE SHOULD, uh, KNOW ABOUT... WELL...

IT'S NO BIG SECRET THAT SOMETHING IS WEIRD ABOUT MERMIN! I MEAN, JUST LOOK AT HIM!

YEAH... HI GUYS. RIGHT HERE.

IT...IT'S TRUE THAT MERMIN IS THE CHILD OF MER ROYALTY!

IN FACT, HIS FATHER IS THE KING, AND MINE IS THE ROYAL ADVISOR!

HE AND I GREW UP TOGETHER, TO INHERIT THE ROLES OF OUR FATHERS--
WRONG!
WHAT BENNI ISN'T MENTIONING IS THAT I HAVE AN OLDER BROTHER WHO WILL BECOME KING!

SO, I'M NOT AS MUCH OF A "PRINCE" AS...

..."A PRINCE'S BROTHER!"

GLAD WE GOT THAT CLEARED UP! HM HM♫

BUT MERMIN...

LOOK AT THIS WEIRD THING I FOUND!
PBTH!

C'MON, PENNY! SHOW ME AROUND THIS PLACE!!

WELL, WELL, WELL! LOOK WHAT WE HAVE HERE!

LOOKS LIKE THE DORK SQUAD IS GROWING!
HA HA HA

PENNY, I DIDN'T KNOW YOU WERE FRIENDS WITH THESE DWEEBS!

YEAH? WHAT OF IT?

NUTHIN'. JUST SURPRISED TO SEE YOU IS ALL.

FINE. WHATEVER. JUST GET OUT OF HERE...

Oh! I GUESS PENNY THINKS SHE'S SO TOUGH NOW THAT SHE'S FRIENDS WITH A MUTANT!
GUESS SO!
Heh! Heh!

YOU WANT A FIGHT? YOU GOT IT! RIGHT, MERMIN?
OKAY!

ALRIGHT! THAT'S ENOUGH OF THAT!
YOU TWO ARE COMING WITH ME!

WHERE ARE WE GOING, PETE?
YEAH, WHAT'S THE PLAN?

WE GO FAR AWAY, GO HOME, AND MOVE ON WITH OUR LIVES.

WAIT-- WE'RE RUNNING AWAY!?!

MERMIN'S TOO STRONG! HE SHOULDN'T FIGHT HUMANS...

LET'S SPLIT UP!

CAN'T BELIEVE WE LOST IT...
ALMOST HAD 'IM!

WAIT...WHAT'S THAT?

AH-HA!

AGENT BIRD! COME IN! THIS IS AGENT SMITT! I'VE LOCATED THE TARGET!

Oh GREAT! YOU GONNA WRAP IT UP IN TISSUE PAPER AND HOPE THAT HOLDS?

VERY FUNNY!
OR MAYBE YOU FOUND SOME COBWEBS THAT IT COULD STEP IN?

WELL, IT'S HEADING YOUR WAY, SO YOU BETTER SET UP YOUR MIRACLE TRAP!

OKAY! THEY'RE HEADING INTO THE PARK NOW!

AWRIGHT! AWRIGHT! I'M JUST CAMOUFLAGING THE TRAP A BIT MORE...

NOW, QUIET DOWN! Hm... WHERE'D I PUT THAT REMOTE...?

THERE WE GO! ALL SET...

(not yet...)

(mm...not sure about that one...)

(NOW!!!)
CLICK!

. . .

WHAT!? HOW COULD THAT NOT HAVE GONE OFF? I BUILT IT MYSELF!
CLICK! CLICK! CLICK! CLICK! CLIC CLICK

WEEN SNAP!
AUGH!

OH NO NO
NO!!

DON'T WORRY LITTLE
GUY! WE'LL GET YOU--

WOBBLE WOBBLE

FLOP!

HM.

Heh!

HA HA HA
NOTHING TO SEE HERE, KID! RUN ALONG! NO NEED TO TELL YOUR PARENTS!
GREAT JOB ON THE TRAP, BIRD.

LISTEN, SMITT! THERE MAY HAVE BEEN SOME MINOR CONSTRUCTION ISSUES...
IS THAT RIGHT!?

WOAH! WOAH! GUYS!! HOLD ON!

ARE... YOU... TRYING TO CAPTURE MERMIN?

uh...
...PERHAPS...

THEN I THINK WE HAVE A LOT TO TALK ABOUT...

CHAPTER FOUR

I CAN'T WAIT TO SHOW CLAIRE THE NEW CLUB HQ TOMORROW!
YEAH, HOPE SHE LIKES IT...

TOBY STILL SEEMED PRETTY MAD AT CLAIRE...
MAYBE THIS'LL SMOOTH THINGS OUT...

REALLY?

YEAH, I GUESS I DON'T KNOW WHAT IT'S LIKE TO HAVE A BROTHER OR SISTER...
Mm.

TELL ME ABOUT YOUR BROTHER, MERMIN.

Oh, WE DON'T HAVE TO GET INTO THAT RIGHT NOW...

M-MAYBE IT WOULD BE BEST TO JUST TELL PETE ABOUT--

MAYBE IT WOULD BE BEST FOR YOU TO NOT BE ALL UP IN MY BUSINESS ALL THE TIME, BENNI!

C'MON, MERMIN... I WANT TO KNOW ABOUT YOU, YOUR FAMILY...

ARGH! I FEEL SURROUNDED!

SIGH FINE... STILL, IT'S CRAZY TO THINK THAT I HAVE A PSYCHIC LINK TO THE PRINCE OF THE SEA.

WELL, YOU CAN'T SEEM TO GET IT TO WORK, SO NO LINK THERE!

MM . . . MAYBE SO . . .

OKAY, GOOD NIGHT, GUYS.

ガンチュラ
Z
Z

AAAAAAHHHHH

Oh, MERMIN. YOU'RE UP!

GOOD MORNING!

C'MON... DON'T GIVE ME THAT LOOK...
Rub Rub

IT'S SATURDAY!

AFTER SOME MANDATORY CARTOONS, WE'LL MEET UP WITH EVERYBODY AND GO BACK TO THE NEW HQ!

WHERE'S BENNI?

WHO WANTS WAFFLES!?

HERE THEY COME!

HI GUYS!

MERMIN... YOU DOIN' OKAY?

I THINK HE, uh, DIDN'T GET MUCH SLEEP LAST NIGHT...

(in fact, it's probably not a good idea to bring up the whole prince thing...)

Oh, DEAR...

I-I'M REALLY SORRY ABOUT YOUR TREE HOUSE...
YEAH, DAD'S GONNA HELP FIX IT, BUT IT'LL TAKE SOME TIME...

IN THE MEANTIME, WE HAVE A NEW, COOL SPOT FOR OUR CLUB MEETINGS!

PENNY'S SUPPOSED TO MEET US THERE!
COME ON!

SO, WHAT DO YOU THINK?
MM... DOESN'T SEEM VERY SAFE...

WHAT!?
AW...

THERE'S JUST A BUNCH OF RUSTY METAL AND STUFF...

YEAH, SORRY. I DEFINITELY DON'T THINK YOU KIDS SHOULD PLAY OUT HERE...

YOU'VE GOTTA BE KIDDING!!

TOBY...

WE WERE HERE YESTERDAY, WHILE YOU WERE WITH YOUR DUMB FRIENDS AND NOTHING BAD HAPPENED!!!

OOOOhhhh...! DOES BABY WANT TO CRY ABOUT IT!?!

ANOTHER PROBLEM WITH THIS PLACE IS THAT RANDY KNOWS ABOUT IT.

Oh, I'M NOT THE ONLY ONE WHO KNOWS ABOUT THIS PLACE...

WHO ARE THESE JERKS?
uh...WELL, THAT'S RANDY. I DUNNO WHO THE OTHER...

HEY! IT'S THAT FISHERMAN!

I AM NOT A FISHERMAN!
I'M AN AGENT OF A PARANORMAL INVESTIGATION UNIT!!

WOAH! WHAT TEAM?!
ARE YOU PART OF THE FBI?

WE'RE JUST STARTING OUT, OKAY? GETTING OUR FEET IN THE DOOR, Y'KNOW?

YOU DON'T HAVE A NAME?
NO COOL ACRONYM?

WE'RE WORKING ON IT!!!

THE POINT IS... THESE GUYS THINK FISHFACE IS AN "EXTRA TERRESTRIAL!"

AND YOU ARE JUST WHAT THEY NEED TO MAKE IT BIG!
rub
rub

WELL...YOU'RE GONNA NEED MORE THAN A NET TO CATCH ME!
Heh!

"MORE THAN A NET," huh?

CHUG
CHUG
CHUG
CHUG

CHUG
CHUG
CHUG
CHUG
CHUG
CHUG
THUNK!

CHUG
CHUG
CHUG
CHUG
Oh, WE'VE GOT SOMETHING BETTER THAN A NET...

CHAPTER FIVE

THIS BETTER BE GOOD...

WHOOSH!
GO!!!

WOOOOOAAAAH...
WHAT THE HECK IS THAT!?
I...I DON'T...
...
CRASH!

CHUG
CHUG
CHUG
CHUG

WELL! WE HAVE TO GET OUTTA HERE!

WAIT!

IS THAT... A BATH TUB?

YEAH...AND I SEE A REFRIGERATOR, AND...

WE BUILT THIS ON A LIMITED BUDGET, OKAY!?!

HEYYY... YOU'RE RIGHT! IT'S JUST A BUNCH OF OLD JUNK!
BIG BATH TUB THOUGH!
uh-huh.

"A BUNCH OF OLD JUNK," HUH!?!

BAM!
RRGH! MISSED!
WAAUGH!!!

THESE GUYS ARE GONNA CAPTURE YOU AND FIND OUT WHAT YOU REALLY ARE!

ALRIGHT, I'LL GET THE LITTLE ORANGE ONE IF YOU CAN CATCH "MERMIN!"

WHAT??

C'MON, BENNI!

YOU'RE MINE, ALIEN SCUM!!

"ALIEN?"
CLANG
THEY THINK YOU'RE FROM ANOTHER PLANET!
LIKE "SPACE PRINCE LANDED!"
NOT THAT AGAIN!

WHY CAN'T EVERYONE JUST LEAVE ME ALONE!?!
YES!
TCH!

SMACK
AUGH!
POW!

oof.

THIS IS GONNA BE TOUGHER THAN I THOUGHT...

Oh, MERMIN...

rngh...

THINGS HAVE BEEN CRAZY SINCE YOU ARRIVED, AND I STILL DON'T REALLY KNOW ABOUT YOUR LIFE BEFOREHAND.

CRASH!

MAYBE WE SHOULDN'T HAVE PUSHED SO HARD ABOUT THE "PRINCE" STUFF...
BAN
SLAM
KRAK

POW

I'M SORRY!
KABAM!!!

WHAM
WOAH!
YAAAHH!
AAIIEE!

MERMIN!

SAVE ME!
!

WHAT!?
DASH!

CRASH

WHUD!

YOU DID IT PETE!!

WHAT? NO... **YOU** SAVED US...

THAT'S NOT WHAT I'M TALKING ABOUT!! I MEAN I **HEARD** YOU!!!

...IN MY HEAD!

THINK ABOUT WHAT YOU DID! HOW IT FELT!
REALLY? I WAS...

...WELL, EVERYTHING WAS CRAZY... I WAS REAL SCARED... I GUESS IT... IT WAS LIKE... uhh...

LIKE
THIS?

YES! THAT'S IT!!
I GOT IT! I GOT IT!!

OKAY, YOU GUYS ARE SERIOUSLY WEIRDING ME OUT RIGHT NOW.

UGH... SORRY YOU KIDS ARE IN THE MIDDLE OF THIS...

BUT IT'S JUST FURTHER EVIDENCE...
...THAT THIS CREATURE IS DANGEROUS!

OKAY. YOU...

...ARE DRIVING ME CRAZY!!

WHOOSH!!!
SMACK!

RAAAHHHH!!!
POW!
BOOM!

HUFF
HUFF
HUFF
HUFF
HUFF

THINK WE LOST HIM?

HE'S GOTTA BE AROUND HERE SOMEWHERE...

LOOKS LIKE THE COAST IS CLEAR!

TOBY, WAIT!

I TOLD YOU! HE'S NOT OUT HERE!!

GAWSH!! YOU'RE A REAL PAIN LATELY, CLAIRE!

ZOOM!
TOBY!!!
SMASH!

HOO!
THAT WAS CLOSE!

CLAIRE... I'M SORRY... I ...
DON'T WORRY ABOUT IT!
few!

I'VE JUST BEEN UPSET... 'CAUSE YOU WANTED TO BE WITH YOUR FRIENDS INSTEAD OF US...

TOBY! I JUST...
YELP!
HUH!?

BENNI!

PUT HIM DOWN!!
HANG IN THERE, BENNI!!

OH NO! THIS ONE'S GOING WITH ME!

YIEEEEE!!!!!
WHA-?
IS THAT...?

I'VE GOT YOUR LITTLE GIRLFRIEND, MERMIN!! GIVE YOURSELF UP!

MAN, WHAT IS IT WITH YOU BULLIES AND "GIRLFRIENDS?"

DON'T WORRY, PENNY! I'LL SAVE YOU!!

AGENT BIRD! I GOT MINE!!

BENNI!!!

UGH! GOOD ENOUGH!!

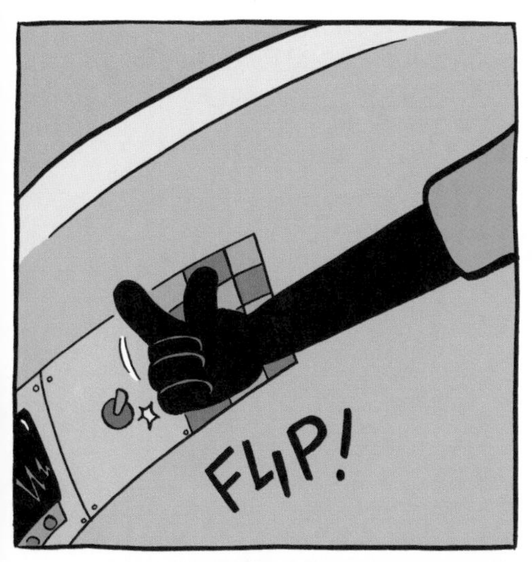
FLIP!

POP!

BENNI!!!

ARGH!
WO-O-O-OAH!
HOLD ON LITTLE GREEN GUY!

WE'RE KEEPING THE GIRL TOO! SMACKING **ME** AROUND IS JUST GONNA HURT **THEM**!

HA HA HA!
LOOK FOR US IN THE SCIENCE BOOKS!
LEAP!

HUH!?!

SO...YEAH... GUESS I'M JUST GONNA GO...

PETE!! WHAT'S GOING ON!?

uh, WELL...uh...
...MERMIN...? WHAT ARE WE GONNA--

BWOOSH!!

GRAB!
Eh?

SLAM!

YOU'RE NOT GOING ANYWHERE!

PENNY!
BENNI!

WE'RE FINE!
OURR NAMEZ ZOUND THE ZAAAME...

Bubble
Bubble

SHOOM!

WHAWHAWHAWHAWHAWHAWHA

MAK!? WHY ARE YOU HERE!?!

HOW MANY OF THESE CREATURES ARE THERE?

THINGS JUST WENT FROM BAD TO WORSE...
C'MON, PEOPLE... ONE FIGHT AT A TIME...

CLANG

KRAK
TOSS!

OKAY, MERMIN...

...THEY'RE ALL YOURS!

CRACK!
POP!

A-AGENT BIRD...?
D-DON'T WORRY, SMITT... I ALMOST HAD 'IM...THIS ISN'T OVER YET...
I THINK IT IS.

SKIIIIID!
KLUNK!
TAP!
Ah-heh...

MERMIN! YOU DID IT!!
HOORAY!!
SO... SLEEPY...

...BUT DON'T FALL ASLEEP YET!
TOO LATE. zZzZz

DON'T WORRY. I'M NOT HERE FOR A FIGHT.

YOU'RE NOT?
HOW DID YOU KNOW WE NEEDED HELP?

I DIDN'T... I JUST ARRIVED AND FOUND YOU IN TROUBLE!
BY THE GREAT DEPTHS, KIDS! IT'S ONLY BEEN A FEW WEEKS...

I CAME HERE FOLLOWING BENNI'S REPORTS.

Y-YES...AS INSTRUCTED I-I'VE BEEN MAKING REGULAR REPORTS TO MER THROUGH FISH NETWORKS...

THE LAST TIME I CHECKED IN WAS JUST BEFORE THOSE GUYS ARRIVED!

Heh. WOW.

SO... WHY **ARE** YOU HERE?
I'M HERE TO DELIVER A MESSAGE...

...THE SITUATION WITH ATLANTIS IS ESCALATING. MERMIN MUST RETURN TO HIS KINGDOM IMMEDIATELY.

Joey Weiser's comics have appeared in several publications including *SpongeBob* Comics and the award-winning *Flight* series. His debut graphic novel, *The Ride Home*, was published in 2007 by AdHouse Books, and the first *Mermin* graphic novel was published in 2013 by Oni Press. He is a graduate of the Savannah College of Art & Design, and he currently lives in Athens, Georgia with his wife Michele and their cat Eddie.

MERMIN™
SKETCHES
glass dome
Joystick controls
Bath tub
is that a bath tub?
We built this on a limited budget, ok!?!
MERMIN BOOK 2

MERMIN
Book 2
Agent Bird
Agent Smith

OTHER BOOKS FROM ONI PRESS

MERMIN, VOL. 1: OUT OF WATER
By Joey Weiser
152 Pages, 6" x 9", Color
ISBN 978-1-934964-98-9

CROGAN'S VENGEANCE
By Chris Schweizer
192 Pages, Hardcover, B/W
ISBN 978-1-934964-06-4

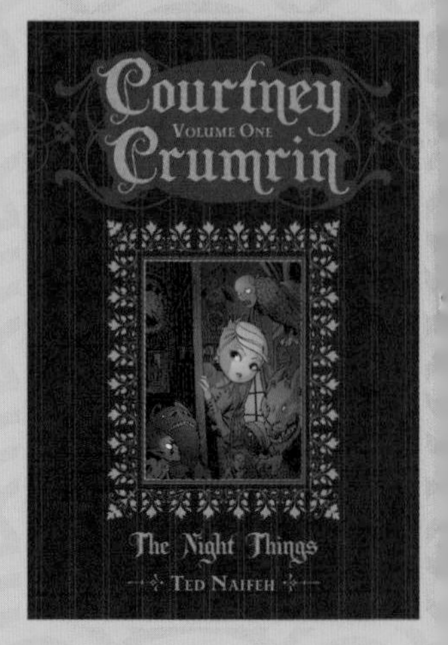

COURTNEY CRUMRIN, VOL. 1: THE NIGHT THINGS
By Ted Naifeh
136 Pages, Hardcover, Color
ISBN 978-1-934964-77-4

POWER LUNCH
By J. Torres & Dean Trippe
40 Pages, Hardcover, Color
ISBN 978-1-934964-70-5

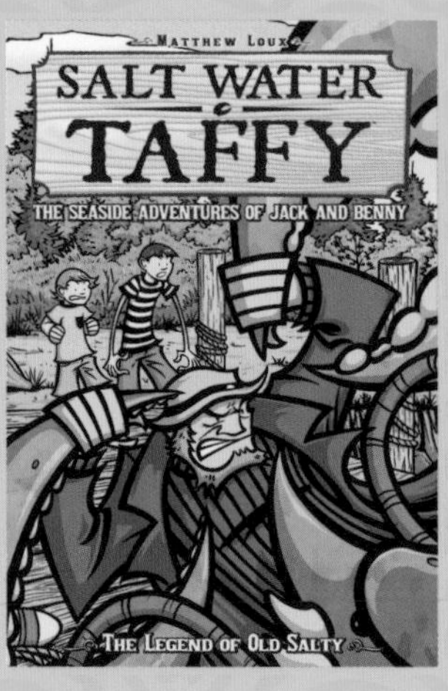

SALT WATER TAFFY, VOL. 1: THE LEGEND OF OLD SALTY
By Matthew Loux
96 Pages, Digest, B/W
ISBN 978-1-932664-94-2

SKETCH MONSTERS, VOL. 1: ESCAPE OF THE SCRIBBLES
By Joshua Williamson & Vinny Navarrete
48 Pages, Hardcover, Color
ISBN 978-1-934964-69-9

For more information on these and other fine Oni Press comic books and graphic novels visit onipress.com. To find a comic specialty store in your area visit comicshops.us.

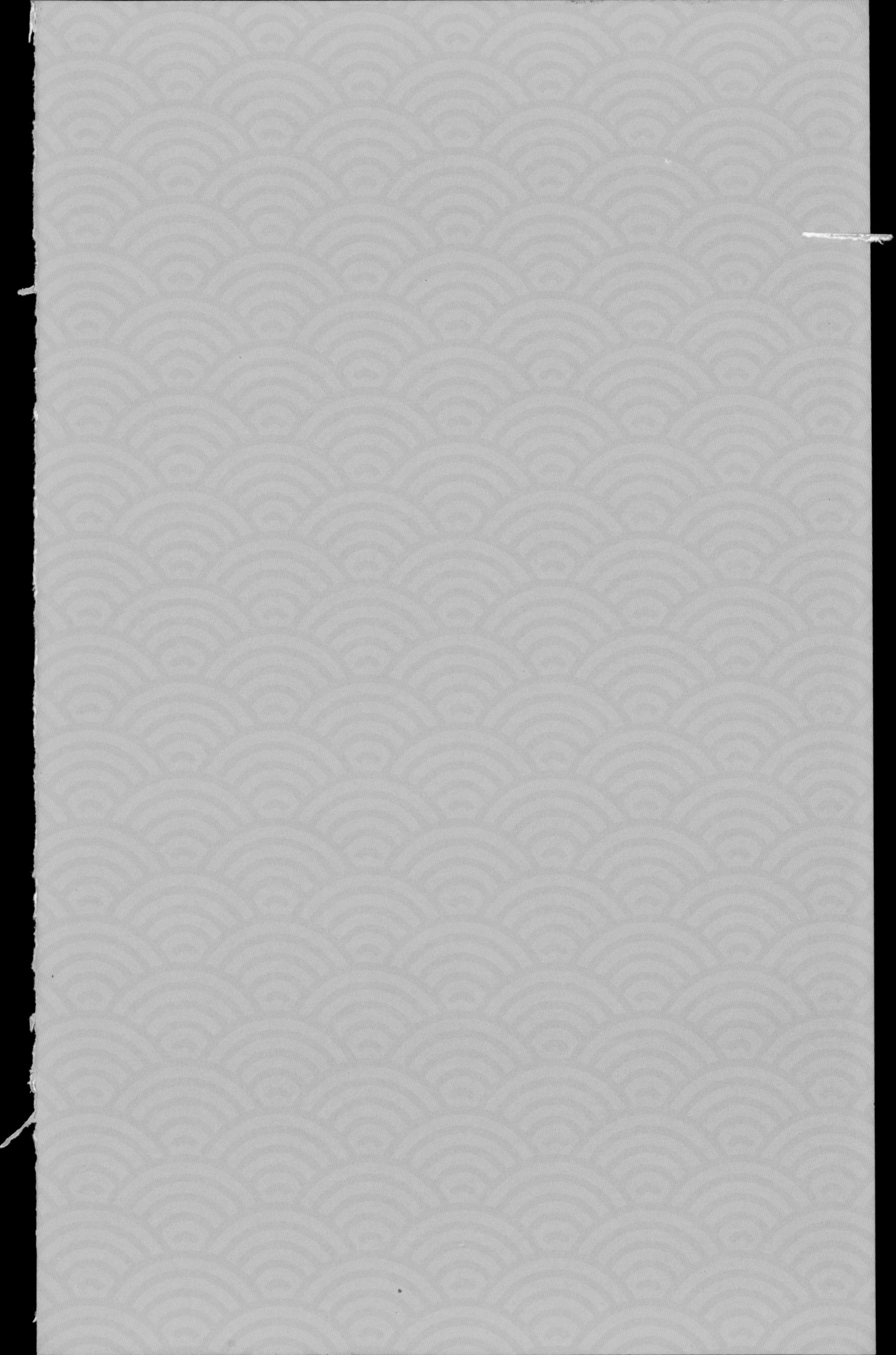